Body Fuel for Healthy Bodies
Dairy Foods

Trisha Sertori

Marshall Cavendish
Benchmark
New York

This edition first published in 2009 in the United States of America by Marshall Cavendish Benchmark.

Marshall Cavendish Benchmark
99 White Plains Road
Tarrytown, NY 10591
www.marshallcavendish.us

First published in 2008 by
MACMILLAN EDUCATION AUSTRALIA PTY LTD
15–19 Claremont Street, South Yarra 3141

Visit our website at www.macmillan.com.au or go directly to www.macmillanlibrary.com.au

Associated companies and representatives throughout the world.

Copyright © Macmillan Education Australia 2008

Library of Congress Cataloging-in-Publication Data

Sertori, Trisha.
    Dairy foods / by Trisha Sertori.
        p. cm.– (Body fuel for healthy bodies)
    Includes index.
    ISBN 978-0-7614-3797-0
    1. Nutrition–Juvenile literature. 2. Dairy products–Juvenile literature. I. Title.
    TX355.S42 2009
    641.3'7–dc22
                                                    2008026022

Edited by Margaret Maher
Text and cover design by Stella Vassiliou
Page layout by Stella Vassiliou
Photo research by Claire Francis
Illustrations by Toby Quarmby, Vishus Productions, pp. 4, 5; Jeff Lang and
    Stella Vassiliou, pp. 8, 9, 10; Stella Vassiliou pp. 22–23.

Printed in the United States

Acknowledgments
The author and publishers are grateful to the following for permission to reproduce copyright material:

Cover and header photos courtesy of © iStockphoto.com (blue cheese); © iStockphoto.com/Galina Barskaya (girl); © iStockphoto.com/Paul W Brain (bottle milk); © iStockphoto.com/Kristian Sekulic (boy); © iStockphoto.com/Khanh Trang (glass milk); © iStockphoto.com/Mykola Velchko (swiss cheese); Stella Vassiliou (bowl & cheeses).

Photos courtesy of:
Artville/Burke Triolo Productions, **28** (bottom); Brand X Pictures, **11** (left); © Hermann Danzmayr/Dreamstime.com, **17** (middle right); © Joe Gough/ Dreamstime.com, **29** (middle); © Franz Pfluegl/Dreamstime.com, **16**; © Nikolaj Tuzov/Dreamstime.com, **29** (2nd bottom); © DW Stock Picture Library, **28** (top); © DW Stock Picture Library/K.Manns, **25** (middle); Getty Images/Dave King, **7** (top); Getty Images/Reza, **23** (bottom left); Getty Images/Ami Vitale, **22** (bottom left); © iStockphoto.com, **25** (top); © iStockphoto.com/Paul W Brain, **1, 3**; © iStockphoto.com/Rob Cruse, **6** (top); © iStockphoto.com/Sergei Didyk, **6** (bottom); © iStockphoto.com/Elena Elisseeva, **7** (3rd top); © iStockphoto.com/Bulent Ince, **8, 9, 10** (right); © iStockphoto.com/Marina Kravchenko, **18**; © iStockphoto.com/Aleksandr Lobanov, **28** (2nd bottom); © iStockphoto.com/Juan Monino, **29** (top); © iStockphoto.com/Greg Nicholas, **7** (bottom); © iStockphoto.com/Bob Randall, **12** (right); © iStockphoto.com/Diane Rutt, **28** (middle); © iStockphoto. com/Arjan Schreven, **22** (middle left); © iStockphoto.com/Suzannah Skelton, **29** (2nd top); © iStockphoto.com/Richard Stanley, **24**; © iStockphoto. com/Bojan Tezak, **20** (top); © iStockphoto.com/Jan Tyler, **21** (bottom); © iStockphoto.com/Wouter Van Caspel, **10** (left); © iStockphoto.com/Liz Van Steenburgh, **17** (middle left); MEA Photos/Lesya Bryndzia, **7** (2nd top & 2nd bottom); Photolibrary/Marc Anderson/Alamy, **23** (bottom right); Photolibrary/John Bavosi/Science Photo Library, **13**; Photolibrary/Anthony Blake Photo Library, **7** (3rd bottom); Photolibrary/David Burton/Alamy, **30**; Photolibrary@David J. Green—food themes/Alamy, **19**; Photolibrary/Martin Lee/Alamy, **28** (2nd top); Photolibrary/Leonard Lessin, **26** (top); Photolibrary/ Pablo Paul/Alamy, **29** (bottom); Photolibrary/David Pearson/Alamy, **23** (top); Photolibrary/Chuck Pefley/Alamy, **26** (bottom); Stephenie Hollyman/Saudi Aramco World/PADIA, **22** (right); © Junial Enterprises/Shutterstock, **27** (bottom); © Patricia Malina/Shutterstock, **22** (top left); Suzanne Tucker/Shutterstock, **17** (bottom); Stockbyte, **14**; Stockbyte/George Doyle, **15**.

MyPyramid symbols courtesy of U.S. Department of Agriculture.

While every care has been taken to trace and acknowledge copyright, the publisher tenders their apologies for any accidental infringement where copyright has proved untraceable. Where the attempt has been unsuccessful, the publisher welcomes information that would redress the situation.

1 3 5 6 4 2

Contents

Glossary Words

When a word is printed in **bold**, you can look up its meaning in the Glossary on page 31.

What Is Body Fuel?

Body fuel is the energy, vitamins, and minerals we need to live. Just as cars need gasoline and computers need electricity, people need energy, vitamins, and minerals to work.

The best way to fuel our bodies is with a **balanced diet**. A balanced diet gives us all the **nutrients** our bodies need.

Nutrients in Foods

The nutrients in foods are divided into macronutrients and micronutrients.

Macronutrients provide energy. They are proteins, carbohydrates, and fats and oils. Micronutrients help **chemical reactions** take place in the body. They are vitamins and minerals.

The Food Pyramid

The food pyramid lists foods for healthy bodies. The colors shown (from left to right) are for grains, vegetables, fruit, oils, dairy, and meat and beans.

MyPyramid.gov
STEPS TO A HEALTHIER YOU

Dairy Foods

Dairy foods are made up of the three macronutrients: carbohydrates, protein, and fat. All dairy foods are made from milk or cream.

Dairy foods are also an excellent source of micronutrients, such as the mineral calcium. Calcium is essential for good health and strong bones, and is an important mineral from dairy foods.

The Food Pyramid

Dairy foods are found in the blue part of the food pyramid. Dairy foods can be high in animal fats, so people should choose low-fat dairy products. People need to eat two to five servings of calcium-rich foods, such as dairy foods, every day. Young children need two to three servings a day. Children and adolescents between ages nine and eighteen need four servings daily. Milk with cereal, a cheese sandwich, a low-fat milkshake, and a container of yogurt equal about three servings of dairy foods.

Body Fuel Health Tips

Cows' milk contains nearly all the important nutrients humans need, including high-quality protein, calcium, vitamin A, vitamin B12, and zinc.

Milk Group
Get your calcium-rich foods

MyPyramid.gov

What Types of Dairy Foods Are There?

The most common type of dairy food is milk from cows. However, people around the world also get milk from other animals, such as sheep, goats, and buffalo. Many different types of dairy foods are made from the milk of these animals.

Milk

Milk mostly comes from dairy farms with hundreds of cows that produce milk. The milk is sent to factories to be processed by homogenization (hom-*oj*-en-ize-*ay*-shun) and pasteurization (*past*-yer-ize-*ay*-shun). Homogenization mixes the milk and cream together. Pasteurization sterilizes milk to remove any harmful **bacteria**. Skim milk is milk that has had the fat removed.

Cheese

Cheese is made by letting milk **curdle**. The soft **curd** is then separated from the watery liquid, called whey, which is left over. There are hundreds of different types of cheeses. Feta cheese is made from goats' milk and sheep's milk. There are also low-fat cheeses made from skim milk, such as cottage cheese and ricotta cheese.

Fabulous Body Fuel Fact

The children's rhyme "Little Miss Muffet" tells us that people once ate curds and whey. Curds and whey are rich in protein, so Miss Muffet was eating terrific body fuel!

Cream
Cream is the thick, fatty part of milk. It floats on top of milk that has not been homogenized.

Buttermilk
Buttermilk is the watery liquid left over after cream has been made into butter. Buttermilk is delicious in pancakes, but is more often used in food for animals.

Yogurt
Yogurt is made from milk that has special bacteria added to it. The bacteria make the milk into a curd and give it a sour flavor.

Powdered milk
Whole milk or skim milk can be dried so that it can be stored for a long time. Dried milk can be mixed with water to make it into a liquid again.

Evaporated milk
Evaporated milk is milk with some of its water removed. Evaporated milk usually comes in cans and can be stored for long periods.

Ice cream
Ice cream is made by stirring cream as it freezes. Fruit, sugar, and flavors are often added to ice cream.

The Digestive System

The digestive system breaks down the foods we eat so they are ready to be absorbed into the bloodstream. Each part of the digestive system plays a part in breaking down, or digesting, foods. **Saliva** and **digestive enzymes** prepare to digest foods even before we eat them. They are produced when we see or smell foods.

Esophagus
The bolus travels down the esophagus (ee-*soff*-a-gus) to the stomach.

Liver
The liver filters nutrients from the blood. Nutrients are sent to the small intestine for digestion. Waste is sent to the large intestine.

Gallbladder
The gallbladder stores bile, which is a digestive liquid made by the liver. Bile is used in the small intestine to break down fats.

Small Intestine
The small intestine is almost 23 feet (7 meters) long. Foods are digested in the small intestine after they are broken down in the stomach. Most nutrients are absorbed into our bloodstream through **villi** in the small intestine.

Mouth
Teeth cut and grind food into smaller pieces. The enzymes in saliva start to break down carbohydrates in the food. The chewed food becomes a **bolus**, which is pushed down the throat by the tongue when we swallow.

Stomach
Stomach muscles churn the bolus. Acid in the stomach makes the food watery.

Pancreas
The pancreas makes enzymes that break down macronutrients.

Large Intestine
The large intestine is 5 feet (1.5 meters) long. It carries waste to the **rectum** for **evacuation** as **feces** (*fee*-seas).

Fabulous Body Fuel Fact

A bolus takes about three seconds to reach your stomach after it is swallowed.

How Does the Body Digest Dairy Foods?

The macronutrients in dairy foods are all digested differently. The macronutrients in milk are made from:

- lactose (carbohydrate)
- casein (*cas*-een) and whey (protein)
- globules of fat, which are inside a special membrane that prevents them from sticking together.

Micronutrients in dairy foods such as calcium do not need to be digested. They are small enough to be absorbed immediately.

Lactose

Lactose is digested in the small intestine. The body makes an enzyme called lactase that breaks down lactose in the small intestine. Lactose must be broken down before it can be absorbed into the bloodstream.

Protein

The digestion of protein from dairy foods begins in the stomach. Protein-busting enzymes called peptides are released in the stomach. Milk is also curdled by stomach acid. Curdling allows the food to stay longer in the stomach so more nutrients can be absorbed as body fuel.

Fats

The fats in dairy foods are digested in the stomach and small intestine. Fats are churned in the stomach and broken into smaller pieces. In the small intestine, an enzyme called lipase breaks the fats down for absorption.

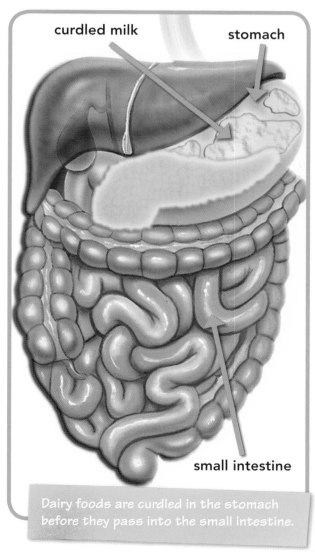

curdled milk

stomach

small intestine

Dairy foods are curdled in the stomach before they pass into the small intestine.

How Does the Digestive System Absorb Dairy Foods?

After food has been digested, it is absorbed into the bloodstream. There are three parts to the small intestine: the duodenum (do-*ah*-de-num), the jejunum (jeh-*joo*-num), and the ileum (*ill*-ee-um). The digestive system absorbs most nutrients in dairy foods through villi in the ileum and jejunum. The nutrients travel through the villi to the blood. Blood carries the nutrients to all the **cells** in the body.

Energy from fat is used during exercise or hard work, such as digging.

Storing Nutrients

When we absorb food, only some of the nutrients are used immediately. Other nutrients are stored so the body can use them later.

Fat

Fat is stored in the liver and under the skin. The body uses this fat for energy during hard exercise or manual work.

Calcium

Calcium is stored in teeth and bones to give them structure and strength.

Other Nutrients

The body also stores other nutrients in the liver, such as glucose, vitamins, and minerals. These nutrients are released when the body needs extra energy.

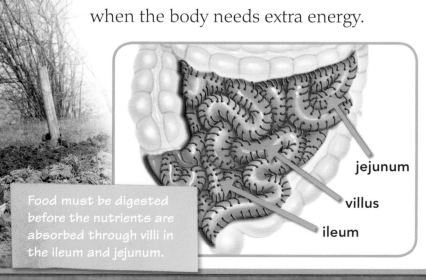

jejunum

villus

ileum

Food must be digested before the nutrients are absorbed through villi in the ileum and jejunum.

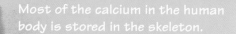

How Dairy Foods Help the Body Function

When dairy foods are absorbed by the body they help the cells in bones, hair, and nails to function.

Bones

Cells in healthy bones are densely packed together. This makes the skeleton strong enough to support the rest of the body. As children grow, calcium helps their bones grow strong. If children do not get enough calcium their bones may become brittle and break easily in adulthood. Calcium from dairy foods is easily absorbed by the body.

Hair and Nails

The body also depends on calcium and zinc from dairy foods for healthy hair and fingernails. Hair and fingernails are made from keratin, which is a hard protein mixed with calcium and zinc.

Body Fuel Health Tips

Soft cheeses, such as ricotta, do not have very much calcium. Do not include them when you count your daily servings of dairy food.

Fabulous Body Fuel Fact

Without the protein called casein, milk would look like water. Casein makes milk white and a little bit thick.

What Nutrients Are in Dairy Foods?

Some important nutrients in dairy foods are vitamins, such as vitamin A, and minerals, such as calcium.

Nutrients	Whole Milk	Cream	Skim Milk	Hard Cheese	Cottage Cheese	Yogurt	Ice Cream	Soy Milk
Macronutrients								
carbohydrate	•	•	•	•	•	•	•	•
protein	•	•	•		•	•	•	•
fats and oils	•	•			traces	•	•	•
Micronutrients								
Vitamins								
vitamin A	•	•	•	•	•	•	•	•
vitamin B2	•	•	•	•	•	•	•	•
vitamin B12	•	•	•	•	•	•	•	
Minerals								
calcium	•	•	•	•	•	•	•	•
magnesium	•	•	•	•	•	•	•	
phosphorous	•	•	•	•	•	•	•	
potassium	•	•	•	•	•	•	•	
zinc	•	•	•	•	•	•	•	

Table: Nutrients in Dairy Foods

People can eat many different kinds of dairy foods for important nutrients, such as calcium.

Body Fuel Health Tips

Calcium and zinc are needed in the chemical reaction that makes energy in the body. They are **catalysts** during the production of energy from glucose.

How Does the Body Use These Nutrients?

Many reactions occur in cells as the body absorbs nutrients through the bloodstream. Blood carries energy, vitamins, and minerals to cells throughout the body, helping the body to function.

Healing
Zinc helps the body heal wounds, such as cuts and bruises.

Brain
Zinc is essential for healthy brain function.

Eyes
Vitamin A is needed for healthy eyesight.

Blood and Muscles
Muscles need calcium to function. Vitamin B12 is needed for healthy blood.

Nerves
Nerves need calcium for healthy functioning. Potassium helps nerves communicate with the brain. Vitamin B12 helps new nerve cells grow.

Bones
Calcium is essential for human bones and teeth to grow and stay strong. Magnesium and phosphorous are also essential minerals in bone development.

Energy Release
Riboflavin helps the body obtain energy from macronutrients.

Fueling the Body with Dairy Foods

Dairy foods are ideal to fuel the human body. They are packed with vitamins, minerals, and energy needed by the body to function well.

Energy

Dairy foods provide easily absorbed energy from carbohydrates for daily activity. The fat in dairy foods is very high in energy. However, the body must convert this fat before using the energy it contains.

Protein

The protein in dairy foods supplies cells with essential nutrients needed for renewal. Protein also helps the body produce enzymes and blood.

Vitamins and Minerals

The vitamins and minerals in dairy foods do not give the body energy. However, they are needed to change macronutrients into a form your body can use. For example, magnesium and calcium help convert glucose into energy.

The protein in dairy foods helps build muscles for exercise.

How Many Servings of Dairy Foods Do I Need Daily?

You should eat at least three servings of dairy foods each day. One serving of dairy food could be:

- 8 ounces (240 milliliters) of milk
- 1 ounce (28 grams) one matchbox-sized piece of cheese
- 8 oz (225 g) of yogurt
- 8 oz (225 g) 1/2 cup of ice cream.

The most important nutrient in dairy foods is calcium, because the human skeleton is made from calcium. People of different ages need different amounts of calcium.

Drinking a glass of milk supplies one serving of dairy food.

Daily Calcium Requirements		
Age	Daily Servings	Amount of Calcium
1–3 years	Two servings, such as a glass of milk and a piece of cheese	500 milligrams
4–8 years	Three servings, such as milk with cereal, a container of yogurt, and a slice of cheese	750 milligrams
9–18 years	Four servings, such as low-fat milk with cereal, a container of yogurt, a low-fat milkshake, and a grilled cheese sandwich	1,000 milligrams

Healthy Food Choices

All dairy foods are healthy food choices. They are prepared in many ways. Some are very healthy choices, and some are less healthy. The following table shows some healthy ways to prepare and eat dairy foods.

✔ Healthy Choices	✖ Less Healthy Choices
whole milk	full-fat, sugary, flavored milk
low-fat milk (except for children under two years of age)	processed cheeses, such as some pre-sliced packaged cheeses
low-fat flavored milk	cheese spreads
low-fat smoothie	full-fat, sweetened yogurt
small amounts of cheese, such as cheddar cheese or other hard cheese	some ice cream
low-fat cheeses	cream
yogurt with live bacteria	

There are many different dairy foods, such as probiotic yogurt, that provide extra health benefits.

Fabulous Body Fuel Fact

There are more than five hundred different species of good bacteria in a healthy human digestive system. All these bacteria look different and do different things. Yogurt with live bacteria can help maintain the correct amount of bacteria in the digestive system.

Body Fuel Health Tips

Water is the best thing to drink when you are thirsty. However, a milk drink is a healthier choice than soda or sugar-sweetened drinks.

Whole-milk Dairy Foods

Whole-milk dairy foods are made from milk that has not had any cream removed. They are high in saturated fats. People need only a very small amount of saturated fat. Too much saturated fat in the diet can lead to diseases, such as cancer and heart disease.

Some high-fat dairy foods are:

- milk chocolate
- cream
- whole-fat cheeses
- condensed whole milk
- evaporated whole milk
- caramels
- whole-milk yogurt
- ice cream.

Trans Fats

Some processed dairy foods, such as cheese spreads and processed cheeses, have an ingredient called trans fat. Trans fat is made from polyunsaturated oil that has had the gas hydrogen added. This causes the fat to become saturated. Food researchers suggest trans fats may be very unhealthy in the human diet. Check food labels for trans fats in dairy foods.

Fat-free or low-fat milk are great alternatives to less healthy dairy foods, such as processed cheese and chocolate.

Functional Foods

Many of the foods we eat each day are very good for us. Food scientists call them "functional foods." That is because these foods have ingredients that may improve health and reduce diseases.

Probiotic Yogurt

One type of functional food is probiotic yogurt. This is low-fat, low-sugar yogurt with live bacteria called probiotics. Probiotics help maintain the number of healthy bacteria in the digestive system. Some types of probiotics found in yogurt are:

- lactobacillus
- acidophilus
- bifidus.

Bacteria in the Digestive System

The body has naturally occurring bacteria in the digestive system. These bacteria are needed for healthy digestion. When there are fewer bacteria in the digestive system, it may be harder for a person to digest food. Eating probiotic yogurt helps maintain the numbers of healthy bacteria in the digestive system.

Eating probiotic yogurt gives you essential calcium and helps your digestive system.

Choosing Functional Foods for Health

The foods we eat can influence our health in the future. Long-term health may be improved by choosing healthy foods, such as functional foods. Choosing functional foods can be as simple as checking food labels for nutrients and probiotics.

Some foods have extra nutrients and probiotics added to them. These may give people added health benefits.

Dairy foods sometimes have added:

- calcium, which forms strong bones and teeth
- vitamin D, which helps the body absorb calcium and lowers the risk of diseases, such as **rickets**
- probiotics, which help to maintain healthy bacteria in the digestive system.

Body Fuel Health Tips

Low-fat dairy, as part of a healthy diet, may help prevent colon cancer and diabetes. It may even have a role in maintaining a healthy weight.

Dairy foods, such as yogurt, can sometimes have added nutrients or probiotics.

Naturally Healthy Dairy Foods

Milk is a naturally healthy food that humans and many animals drink when they are young. Milk is high in fat to help babies grow quickly. It is also rich in proteins for cell renewal. Milk also has carbohydrate for the energy needed to fuel the body. Other nutrients in milk, such as potassium and calcium, help babies develop healthy bones and teeth. Older children and adults can choose low-fat dairy products to receive the benefits of dairy foods without the fats.

Many animals, such as cows, drink milk from their mothers when they are young.

Body Fuel Health Tips

For naturally good health, eat low-fat, calcium-fortified dairy foods, such as:

- milk on calcium-fortified cereal
- an 8-ounce (225-gram) container of probiotic yogurt
- a slice of low-fat cheese on multigrain bread.

Calcium Deficiency

When people do not eat enough calcium they are at risk of calcium deficiency. Their bones become weaker and their muscles may not work efficiently.

Storing Calcium

Bones and teeth store 99 percent of the calcium in the body. The rest is used in **muscle contractions**, in **blood clotting**, and to carry messages along nerves. If a person is calcium deficient, the body takes calcium from bones to perform these other functions. This reduces bone strength.

If people do not get enough calcium, their bones may be more likely to break.

Dairy Foods Around the World

Dairy foods are eaten only in some countries around the world. Many people throughout Asia rarely or never eat dairy foods. Dairy is the only food group from the food pyramid that some nations either do not eat or eat very rarely.

The Netherlands
The Netherlands is famous for its cheeses. One of the most famous is gouda. This cheese has little holes, created while the cheese is **curing**.

Greece
Many parts of Greece are dry and rocky with little vegetation. Raising cows on this land is difficult, so the people raise goats and sheep for their dairy foods. One well-known Greek goat and sheep cheese is called feta. Feta is a white, crumbly, salty cheese that is eaten in salads and spinach pies.

Central Africa
The Masai people of Kenya and Tanzania in Central Africa raise cattle for milk and meat. The Masai sometimes make a small cut in a cow's neck to take some blood. The blood is mixed with the cows' milk, which is then drunk. The cut in the cow's neck is plugged with grass to help it heal.

United States

North Africa and the Middle East
The Bedouin people of North Africa and the Middle East milk their camels for dairy foods. The Bedouin farm camels because these animals survive well in the desert.

As you can see from this world map, people around the world eat different kinds of dairy foods. People who do not traditionally eat dairy foods eat other foods that contain calcium.

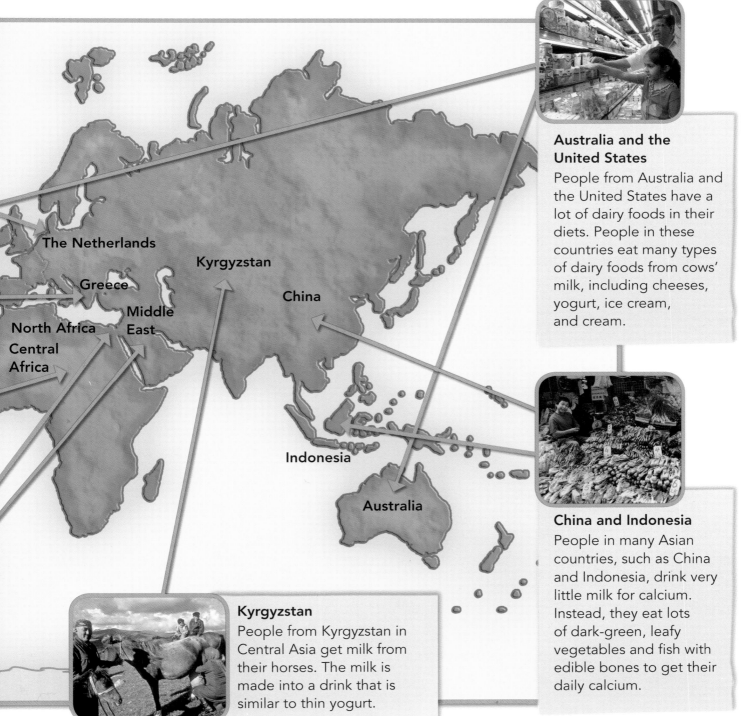

The Netherlands

Kyrgyzstan

Greece

China

Middle East

North Africa

Central Africa

Indonesia

Australia

Australia and the United States
People from Australia and the United States have a lot of dairy foods in their diets. People in these countries eat many types of dairy foods from cows' milk, including cheeses, yogurt, ice cream, and cream.

China and Indonesia
People in many Asian countries, such as China and Indonesia, drink very little milk for calcium. Instead, they eat lots of dark-green, leafy vegetables and fish with edible bones to get their daily calcium.

Kyrgyzstan
People from Kyrgyzstan in Central Asia get milk from their horses. The milk is made into a drink that is similar to thin yogurt.

Allergies and Intolerances to Dairy Foods

Food allergies and intolerances are reactions by our bodies to different foods. A food allergy occurs when the **immune system** reacts as if a food is dangerous. This reaction may cause itchy skin or make breathing difficult. A food intolerance is a negative chemical reaction in the body to the food. These reactions often cause similar symptoms to allergic reactions.

Lactose Intolerance

The most common intolerance to dairy foods is lactose intolerance. People who are lactose intolerant cannot digest milk properly. This is because their bodies do not make the enzyme lactase. Lactase is needed to digest the lactose in dairy foods.

Eczema

Some children get a skin rash called eczema. If children are allergic to casein, the protein in milk, dairy foods can make eczema worse. People who are allergic to casein may need to avoid eating dairy foods.

Some foods that contain casein are:

- enriched cereals
- high-protein beverage powders
- ice cream
- health bars
- processed meats
- salad dressings.

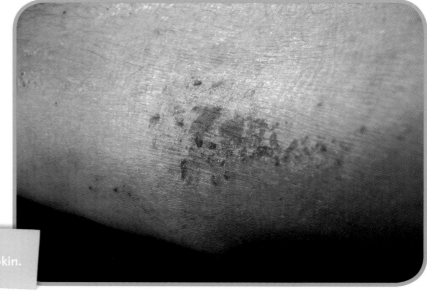

Eczema can cause redness and scabs to appear on a person's skin.

What Can I Eat if I Have a Dairy Intolerance or Allergy?

People who have allergies or intolerances to dairy foods can eat other foods for calcium. These include:

- dark-green, leafy vegetables, such as spinach and bok choy
- fish with edible bones, such as sardines
- soybean products, such as tofu and tempeh
- orange juice and cereals enriched with calcium.

Some fish, such as sardines, have small, soft bones which can be eaten to provide calcium.

Low-lactose Foods

Yogurt and cheese are low in lactose. People with lactose intolerance can eat and digest these foods.

Soy Milk

Dairy foods can also be substituted for calcium-fortified soy milk, which is made from soybeans. It is made into ice cream, flavored milk drinks, cheese, and yogurt.

Soy milk does not have lactose because it is not a dairy product.

Body Fuel Health Tips

Removing dairy foods from the diet leaves a big gap in the supply of nutrients. If you think you are allergic to dairy foods, you can ask to see an allergy specialist.

Checking Food Labels for Dairy Foods

Many manufactured foods or packaged foods have labels that tell us all the ingredients in the food. People read labels to check for any ingredients to which they may have an allergy or intolerance.

Food labels also list the amount of calories from fats, carbohydrates, and proteins in the food, as well as vitamins and minerals. People can compare ingredients in different foods by reading food labels.

Foods with Dairy Ingredients

Dairy foods are listed under many different names on food labels. They are used in many of the packaged foods on supermarket shelves. Check for dairy ingredients in:

- breads
- cookies
- drinks
- spreads
- cakes
- sweets.

The labels on dairy foods show how much protein, fat, and carbohydrates are in the foods.

Ingredients to Avoid

People with dairy allergies or lactose intolerance should avoid foods with these ingredients:

- dried milk powder
- whey
- casein
- milk
- lactose.

People can check food labels to compare the ingredients in different products.

Checking Food Labels for Healthy Eating

Food labels can help us choose the healthiest foods on supermarket shelves. The healthiest dairy foods are high in protein and calcium.

Milk

Whole milk has up to 3.7 percent fat. Low-fat milk has less than 2 percent fat. Different types of milk have the same amount of protein, carbohydrates, and micronutrients, unless they are enriched with added ingredients.

Yogurt

There are many different types of yogurt available. Some are flavored, some plain, and some have added fruit. Compare yogurt food labels and choose low-fat, low-sugar yogurt.

Body Fuel Health Tips

Research shows that milk and milk products might protect your teeth from getting holes and decay. This is because dairy food can reduce acidity in your mouth, stimulate saliva, and reduce plaque formation. So, check labels for terrific low-fat, low-sugar dairy foods for good health.

You can read a food label to make sure the food does not contain too much fat.

Cooking Class

Try these two easy, high-calcium snacks as a healthy after-school treat. These recipes supply:

- carbohydrates for energy
- protein for cell renewal
- fiber and probiotics for healthy digestion
- fats and oils for healthy skin and **cell membranes**
- vitamin A for eyesight
- calcium for strong bones.

low-fat milk

Fruit and Yogurt Smoothie

Servings Two

Preparation time 10 minutes

Ingredients

1 pint (500 milliliters) low-fat milk

1/2 small container of low-fat yogurt with live bacteria

4 strawberries (or other seasonal fruits)

1 banana

1 teaspoon honey

1 heaped teaspoon malt

3 ice cubes (if you like your drinks really cold)

low-fat yogurt

strawberries

Preparation

1. Place all the ingredients in a food processor.

2. Put the lid on and switch the processor to high. Process for about 2 minutes.

3. The smoothie is ready when it looks like a thick milkshake. The fruits and honey should be well mixed.

4. Serve in a big glass.

banana

honey

Easy Cheese Quesadillas

Servings Two
Preparation time 10 minutes
Cooking time 20 minutes

Ingredients

2 teaspoons polyunsaturated oil

2 servings of tortillas/pitas

3/4 cup thinly sliced cooked chicken or ham

3/4 cup grated low-fat cheddar cheese

1/2 cup of whole corn kernels

Preparation

1. Place the oil in a large frying pan over medium heat.

2. Place a tortilla into the warmed pan.

3. Spread ham or chicken over the tortilla.

4. Sprinkle grated cheese over the meat.

5. Add the corn kernels.

6. Cover with the second tortilla and cook slowly until the cheese melts.

7. Serve alone for a snack or add a salad for a light meal.

tortillas

thinly sliced ham

low-fat cheddar cheese

corn kernels

Fueling the Body with Healthy Dairy Foods

Dairy is one of the best food groups for growing children. Dairy foods have lots of the proteins, carbohydrates, and fats needed for healthy growth. But more importantly, dairy foods supply calcium and lots of other essential vitamins and minerals.

Without calcium, our bones and teeth cannot grow properly. If children are calcium deficient, they are at greater risk of broken bones as adults. People can get calcium from non-dairy foods, such as green, leafy vegetables. However, calcium from vegetables is harder for humans to absorb. The calcium from dairy foods is easily absorbed into our bodies.

People need three to five servings of dairy foods each day. This supplies enough calcium for good health. Choosing the right dairy foods is also important. When we choose low-fat, high-protein dairy foods we get lots of good body fuel.

A delicious milk drink is a healthy way to get calcium and other important nutrients.

Glossary

bacteria	tiny living things that live in soil, water, plants, animals, and humans
balanced diet	a mix of different foods that provides the right amount of nutrients for the body
blood clotting	the hardening of blood to form a lump, such as a scab
bolus	a small ball of chewed food
catalysts	substances that speed up chemical reactions
cell membranes	the thin skin that surrounds cells
cells	microscopic structures that combine to make up all the bones, muscles, and other parts of the body
chemical reactions	processes by which substances are changed into other substances
curd	thick, white substance made of casein, the protein in milk
curdle	to change into curd
curing	hardening and preserving through partial drying
digestive enzymes	proteins that speed up the chemical reactions involved in the digestion of food
evacuation	removal from the body
feces	solid waste that is evacuated from the body
immune system	the body system that fights infections
muscle contractions	the movements of muscles as they do work
nutrients	substances that provide energy when eaten
rectum	the end of the large intestine, where feces are stored before evacuation
rickets	a disease of the bones caused by vitamin D deficiency
saliva	the fluid in the mouth that helps digest food
villi	small, fingerlike bumps on the inside wall of the small intestine

Index